Katerina

Katerina

Erik Hofstatter

ROSTITUTES. I never fucked one before, not because of the lack of opportunities (I live in Prague after all) but simply because I possessed a certain set of standards. I was clean, but not always. Chlamydia sneaked up on me once in my capricious youth (not from a hooker, but with her promiscuity she might as well have been one) and I really didn't fancy another trip to the sex clinic. The nurse judging me again with her patronising stare while I'm filling out the form, telepathically telling me that I'm older than most of these kids and that I should've known better. Yeah, alright. I should've known better—but fuck it.

My cunt of an ex-girlfriend swapped me for a career, indelicately breaking my heart in the process, and I embarked on a path of self-destruction, in other words drinking and fucking anything with a pulse—just to get it out of my system. It worked for a while. Until I started pissing out this weird, cloudy discharge. I knew I caught something then and attempted to banish my stupidity by breaking the bathroom tiles with my forehead.

I *really* should've known better but my God, I hate condoms. I slipped one on to begin with, but I just didn't feel a goddamn thing! The rubbery bastard isolated me too much. The fact that she had a parachute instead of a vagina didn't help, either. So I ditched it. Big mistake.

Now in my 30s, I'm more responsible or so I thought. Besides, I'm still young and handsome. Why on Earth would I need to hire a vagina when I can still get one for free? Why do men do it anyway? Most of these pussy-selling wrecks are ridden with diseases, too drunk or high on drugs to even register what's going on half the time.

Is that part of the attraction? Is it because it's fast and discreet? No questions asked? No strings attached? What their spouses don't know won't hurt them kind of thing? A cheeky treat for the penis? Like munching on a burger when you're on a diet? (no pun intended). I often wondered what sort of losers pick up street hookers. Were they the stereotypical bald, sleazy, sweaty, pot-bellied, semi-impotent old men you see in movies?

Guess it comes down to personal taste. I always had a sophisticated palate. I wouldn't poke these sluts with a metre long stick—let alone my cock! I'd rather keep fucking my right hand than one of them. I wasn't desperate for sex. I didn't plan paying for sex.

I drove to my humble flat after work, located in Wenceslas Square (and the Red-Light District part of Prague). I lived there for seven years now and although I was fed up with the hookers, pimps and junkies hanging around it—I had a sentimental attachment to the place. The cosy, spacious rooms, wooden beams connecting the walls, the ornamented ceiling. The flat had a character. I could *smell* the history. The only let down were the locals (and non-locals who came here for stag parties).

And there she was, patrolling the corner—stalking her next prey. Her Denim skirt raised high, no panties underneath to allow easy access (that's a wild guess) black, shiny Cossack boots and that pleading look in her eyes that shouted "Buy me! Buy me! I'm yours!" The very same look she offered to ten other men that night.

The most vital thing to remember is *not* to make an eye contact. If you do, you'll signal your interest and they'll approach or follow you afterwards. I made that mistake before. Now I just blank them every night when I turn corner and drive past. Usually they're transparent to me, nothing more than stains on a wall. But this night was different.

I parked the Skoda outside my flat and emerged from the car.

"Wanna blowjob for 200, hon? The best one you ever had," said a high-pitched voice from behind me.

I dropped the keys, startled.

"No, get out of here." I said in a dismissive tone, bending down and picking the keys up.

"Oh come on, babe. It's just 200 crowns. You're in for a treat," she said, poking her tongue out.

She stood directly underneath the street lamp; I did a double take and saw a brief glimpse of her pierced tongue. I always wanted to sample one of those. Not hookers, we covered that, but a blowjob with a pierced tongue. Apparently, it really was a treat and for 200? That's a bargain for sure. Nowadays you spend that kind of money on a lousy pub lunch, so why not on a stimulating blowjob?

I gave her the once-over. She seemed pretty—younger than the others. Maybe 19? She was slim and petite, not yet ruined by years in the trade. That was my impression anyway. Her ginger hair was tied in a pony-tail (she was sensible at least, there's nothing more annoying than a girl sucking your dick and interrupting it by constantly brushing away hair from her mouth). Her lips were plump, bouncy. Always a plus.

"What's your name?" I asked after my inspection.

"Ginny."

"Like the ginge from *Harry Potter*?"

"No, like my favourite drink," she said, pulling out a bottle of Gin from her tattered handbag.

"Want some?" She offered, taking a quick gulp.

"No thanks. Think I have a pretty good idea where your lips have just been."

She smirked. "Don't be an asshole. You want me to blow you or what?"

"How old are you?"

"Why does it matter? I know what I'm doing. Had plenty of practice and I ain't lying when I say you're in for a treat."

"It matters because you could be like 15. I can't fucking tell these days."

"I'm 20. Want me to show you an ID or something?"

"No."

"You haven't done this before, right?" Ginny asked, "I can tell you're nervous."

She was right of course. What the hell was I doing? Why was I even talking to her still? The prospect of an exotic fellatio excited me somewhat, but the desire seemed deeper than that. There was something about her, something...primal.

"Okay then, let's go," I said.

Ginny nodded and followed me up the steep staircase that led into my abode. I turned the key inside the lock and gave the door a little nudge with the tip of my shoulder. I swear the place shrank with age. We entered the hallway.

I pointed at her footwear. "Boots off,"

"You fucking joking?"

"No, I'm not. This cow rug cost more than your education and I don't want any shit all over it. Boots off," I repeated. She complied.

"I ran out of booze so might have some of that Gin of yours after all. Let me get some glasses," I said, walking into the narrow kitchen. I was too sober for this. I grabbed a couple of shot glasses from the cupboard. Upon my return, I found Ginny standing in the living room and studying one of my medieval axes. She'd taken her jacket off while I was gone.

I now studied the shape of her tits through her Harley Davidson shirt with equal fascination.

"You're not some kind of a murderer, are you?" she asked, tracing her fingertips along the edge of the axe.

"Please, don't touch that. And no, I'm not. I'm a medieval weapons collector and trader, if you must know."

She met my eyes and raised an eyebrow. "Interesting."

"Glad you approve. Now let's see some Gin, er, Ginny."

Ginny produced the half empty bottle from inside her bag and handed it over to me. I drank two shots straight, feeling the potent liquid coursing through my belly. I had to be careful, though, for many reasons. Number one, my dick was useless when I consumed too much alcohol. Some of my friends loved fucking whilst under the influence, Tomas even claimed that it enhanced his performance, making him last longer. But me? Limp as a noodle. And I didn't want to pay 200 for nothing. Number two, I needed to stay in control. There was a strange hooker in my flat. If I passed out, she would probably rob me blind. Come to think of it, bringing her inside my property wasn't the smartest thing I did today. Now she knew where I lived. She could break in when I'm out working.

"What' your real name, Ginny?"

She drank her shot and I poured her another.

"I'd rather not say. Let's keep this clean and professional, yeah? Call me Ginny, that's all you need to know. Now let's see some money. The show must go on and all that."

I removed the wallet from my back pocket. There wasn't much in it. I pulled out a 200 crown note and passed it to her. She folded it into little squares and slid it inside her jacket.

"Thanks very much. Now take off your pants and make yourself comfortable," she said, pointing at the couch.

This felt weird already. Like most men, I was insecure about the size of my equipment. There was a certain taboo in my family when it came to nudity. My best friend, Tomas, grew up on different principles. His father abandoned him during infancy and Tomas was solely raised by his working class mum who, let me tell you, wasn't shy at all. I spent a great deal of my childhood at their house, where Jane (his mum) often hoovered in her underwear, a memory I safely deposited in my teenage wank bank. She often got changed in front of Tomas, sunbathed topless for all to see—that kind of thing.

This interesting parenting approach led to Tomas lobbing his cock out whenever opportunity permitted (including the gym changing rooms where he walked around with it after a shower, waving his fuckstick in my face). I was modest when it came to nudity and always showered home after a workout. I felt violated by the idea alone—sharing a shower with half a dozen of nude, strange men. No thanks.

"Come on then, whatcha waiting for? Oh, I see. You're shyyyy," she said, a mischievous grin forming on her luscious lips.

Ginny slipped her warm hand in mine and led me to the couch. She whipped me around and started unbuttoning my jeans. I trembled. She must've thought I was a virgin, and for a moment—that's what I thought, too. I felt lost! I'd banged plenty of chicks in my past but this was different. It threw me off my game. I grinned whilst she worked the buttons. She smelled of lavender, like a cheap toilet air freshener.

Shit! Should I be squeezing her tits? Nuzzling her hair? Lean in for a kiss? Was that even allowed? The booze clouded my logic. Why else would I feel the desire to kiss a hooker who probably had seven kinds of cock breath?

I attempted to kiss her anyway. She pulled back.

"No kissing. You just gave yourself away, Mister. Now I know you *definitely* haven't done this before."

She yanked down my jeans and boxers, her eyes nearly jumping out of their sockets when she was greeted by my erection. She looked surprised (in a good way).

"Look at the girth!" she said, pushing me into the cushions.

Ginny rearranged her hair. "Now just sit back and enjoy the ride. It will feel like a trip around the world,"

Then she put me in her mouth. Ginny's technique got me hard like never before. Her hands were multitasking, one strategically sliding along the length of my shaft whilst the other cradled my balls. What a talented girl!

She made me groan at first, then I began to produce these weird, orangutan-like noises and before I knew it—I was overwhelmed by a sudden desire to fuck her. Not just her mouth, but every hole in her body.

"How much for a fuck?" I asked, gently lifting her head from my cock.

She wiped her mouth on her arm and studied my expression for a second, as if trying to gauge how much I could afford.

"You can fuck me for 1500, medieval boy."

I laughed. "You're good, but you're not that good!"

"Fuck you!"

"You can, but for less than 1500," I joked.

"How about a thousand then?"

"That's better. Take off your clothes,"

"Money upfront," Ginny said, crossing her arms.

I raised myself from the couch and hopped to the table. I paid her the dough (my wallet was empty now) and watched her undress.

"You got a rubber?" she asked.

"Yeah, in that top drawer behind you," I said.

Honestly? I didn't want to use one but my brush with Chlamydia taught me a harsh lesson. Besides, I could catch a lot worse from a street whore. The condom had to stay on this time. I could only hope her pussy was tight and I would be able to *feel* something. We drank another shot of Gin; it probably helped her to ease the guilt of selling her body, whilst it helped me to stall my ejaculation. You have no idea how much willpower it took not to come in her mouth.

"Where's your bedroom?"

"Let's fuck on the couch; I don't want your filthy body on my sheets," I said.

Ginny dropped her chin then, as if my words wounded her.

"What's the matter?"

"It's nothing. How do you want me?" she asked.

"From behind. Bend over the couch there. No, not that side. The other side,"

She obeyed. I dressed my cock in a nice rubber hat and launched him inside her. Ginny was dry but the lubricant from the condom made her more slippery. I guess they were useful after all. Her buttocks were firm and I groped it, spanked it even at one point. Such a tight ass! This was worth every crown.

My thighs started quaking after few minutes so I decided to let her do some work. I stopped and walked around her, sitting on the couch.

"Come here, earn your money and climb on top," I said.

Ginny didn't answer. She raised her face from between the cushions; it was bright red from having her head bent so low over the couch while I was ramming her from behind. That or it was a ginger thing, I don't know.

She sat on my lap and slowly impaled herself on my erect cock. I rubbed her tits while she pounced on me, slowly at first, and then she found her rhythm and it turned into a full rodeo. We fucked for what seemed like hours and I was completely drenched at the end of it. Ginny collapsed on the couch, sweat dripping from her breasts. I took a swig of the Gin (not caring about drinking from the bottle anymore) and collapsed next to her.

"Did you enjoy my body?" She asked.

I felt my erratic heartbeat pounding.

"You have no idea," I exhaled with my eyes closed. Then I drifted off to sleep with Ginny next to me and the cum-drenched condom still wrapped around my penis.

HE sudden commotion originating from the kitchen disturbed my slumber. I groaned and massaged my aching temples—the hangover began its tortures early. The lamp was still on.

I glanced at the wall clock, trying to focus on the blurry digits—2:56 a.m. — still the middle of the night. What the fuck was going on? Was someone trying to break into the flat? It wouldn't be the first time.

A couple of months ago, two desperate junkies attempted a break in. It was a sunny Sunday, quite early in the morning when I heard knocking on the door. I'm not used to visitors. The only person who ever comes to see me is Tomas, and he wouldn't come over unannounced—he always texts first. The knocking got louder. I tiptoed towards the wall and peeked out of the kitchen window, seeing a man in his late 30s pushing against the door—against *my* door.

I liberated one of the smaller axes off the wall (a short bearded Viking axe to be precise) only a blunt replica, but it could still inflict some damage and swung the door open with uncalculated force.

"What the fuck are you doing?" I demanded.

The junkie's startled eyes slipped toward the axe.

"I…I'm so-rry," he said, stammering.

I noticed a female druggie companion of his, standing below the stairs—keeping a lookout.

"We were j-just looking for the c-church," the male junkie said.

I must admit, his ridiculous excuse caught me off guard. I didn't know whether he was insulting my intelligence or if he was high enough to truly believe that my flat was a church. I believed the former.

"Nice try. Get the fuck out here!" I said.

"Y-yes, sir,"

He was just leaving but I grabbed his shirt anyway and spun him around.

"And if you ever come back here, I'll chop off your fucking hands, got it?" I said. I raised the axe and pointed it at his whore, "That applies to you, too. Now get lost."

They disappeared and never came back. Until now. Maybe.

Something dropped in the kitchen. Then I remembered Ginny. She wasn't on the couch with me.

"Ginny, is that you? What are you doing in there?"

No reply. I got up on my feet. The sudden head rush made me dizzy. I noticed the condom was still wrapped around my cock. I finally took the fucking thing off. Drops of semen landed on the carpet.

"For fuck sake! Ginny! Are you in there?"

No answer. Maybe she woke up earlier in the night and left. I could hardly expect her to stay for a morning cuddle. Not that I wanted her to. Who the fuck was in my kitchen then?

I kept a samurai sword behind one of the curtains (another replica). I reached for it and slid it out of its sheath. Then I crept towards the kitchen. The light was on. I wish it wasn't. Now I can't unsee the horrific scene that unravelled before me. My jaw dropped. I've never seen anything like it. There was blood and loads of it, smeared across the linoleum.

Kneeling on all fours, fully naked was Ginny. Her head bowed low, face covered by her ginger strands of hair; she was devouring something in a small pool of blood. I could not see clearly what she was eating.

"Ginny? What are you doing?" I asked gently, clutching the sword in my hand.

When I moved closer, she hissed at me. When Ginny raised her head, I gasped. A decapitated head of a giant rat lay on the floor whilst she held the headless, partially moving body in her mouth. The tail of the rat still flicked from side to side, blood and entrails dripping from its body. This was a recent kill. Although the rat was huge, I never expected it to hold so much blood. I glimpsed at my set of cooking knives. None of them were missing. Ginny must've ripped the rat's head off with her teeth.

"What the fu—"

Shock paralyzed my legs. I could not move. I stood there for a moment, blinking, watching Ginny lick blood off the rat's severed neck. I blinked again. My wits returned and I put the sword down. I marched into the kitchen, sidestepping the bleeding head and grabbed Ginny by the arm, dragging her out. She continued to hiss and scratch. Her nails were long and dug deep into my flesh, leaving blood trails all over my arms and neck. The sharp pain twisted my face. I could only hope she wasn't HIV positive or infected with rabies.

"What the fuck is wrong with you?" I said, too disturbed to really care about her answer.

I snatched her clothes off the chair and shoved them into her arms whilst dragging Ginny out of the flat. Her claws found my neck again and I had no other choice but to slap her, hard. She kept hissing at me and I finally managed to push her outside, naked and deranged. I slammed the door shut and locked it. I saw her blurry figure through the door glass, putting clothes back on. Then, the clapping of Ginny's boots descending the stairs echoed all around. Thank fuck she was leaving!

Still hyperventilating, I retreated into the bathroom. I turned on the tap and washed my wounds. They burned like hell. In the kitchen, I cleaned up the mess—still unsure what to make of it all. Afterwards, I collapsed on the couch, exhausted. It wasn't easy but sleep found me eventually. What a night.

 HAD a long day at work, driving around and supplying various independent medieval shops with my replica weaponry. All I wanted to do was to crash on the couch, (I cleaned up all the bodily fluids this morning) crack open a cold beer and watch some crap telly. But like most of my life, nothing worked the way I planned. I was approaching the dreaded corner, Ginny's territory, and I felt invisible knots twisting my stomach.

I turned the Skoda into the shady road, relieved to see a different hooker working her corner, and parked my car in the driveway. As I started climbing the stairs, I spotted a dark silhouette leaning against the wall. My heart sank.

"Finally! Where have you been, man? I've been texting and calling."

I recognised the voice immediately and felt like kissing him.

"Tomas! I'm so relieved it's you!"

His expression seemed puzzled. "Who else? Did you forget that nobody likes you and I'm your only friend?"

"Funny. What are you doin' here? It's unlike you to come over uninvited." I said.

"I called *and* texted," he repeated, "but you didn't pick up. Where you been?"

"At work—sorry to inform you, but some of us have to earn a living," I said, searching my pockets, "shit! I was rushing this morning and must've left my mobile in the flat."

Tomas smirked. He still lived at home with his parents at the age of 27. Embarrassing notion and something I could never do, not unless it was a matter of life and death.

"Wanna beer?" I said, unlocking the door.

"Sure thing. How's business then?"

"Not great. There are only so many replicas you can sell in this district. I'm gonna have to broaden my radius and start travelling further."

I got us some beers from the fridge and switched the telly on low volume.

"Where have you been?" I asked, passing Tomas an open bottle.

"Gym. Trained my chest yesterday and shoulders today. I'm so fucking sore," he said, rubbing his bulging shoulder.

I poked him in the chest, just to watch him squirm. He squealed in agony and I laughed.

"You're growing soft, man!"

"Not as soft as you—you're soft as shite!" he said, poking my belly.

"Well, I've had a different type of workout last night, more…cardiovascular," I replied, winking.

I didn't want to reveal too much to Tomas about last night's events. The truth is, Ginny's bizarre behaviour scared me. But I wasn't going to tell *him* that. Besides, we were just measuring dicks now—comparing egos with some manly banter.

"Oh yeah? Who was she?" asked Tomas, sipping his beer.

I scratched my scalp, sweating. I sucked at lying. And he knew it.

"Wait a minute; you didn't fuck a street whore, did you?"

Bastard! He could read me like an open book. I probably had it written across my forehead.

"Eh, kinda," I confessed.

Tomas burst out laughing.

"Ha! I can't believe how you used to preach to me about hookers, the potential risks, how much you hated them, wouldn't go anywhere near them and all that—fucking hypocrite!" He chuckled.

He did have a point and I felt like a douchebag. Tomas *loved* prostitutes. He occasionally worked in a brothel as a bouncer. Working in such an establishment came with certain perks, including free fucks, and he wasn't shy about reaping the benefits. Whether he was in a relationship or not, he could always rely on his whores to keep him happy.

"I didn't fucking plan it. She ambushed me outside my flat!"

"And you just couldn't say no, could you?" Tomas said, still laughing.

"I tried, but there was something about her. She was different…"

She certainly was. How much should I tell him? Ginny was a great fuck but what about the kitchen incident? That sure as hell wasn't normal.

"Different? How? Was she a tranny?" He smirked.

"Fuck off! She was nice and ripe to begin with. Juicy ass with firm tits."

"You hound dog! What was her name? Maybe I know her?"

That didn't occur to me. His expertise was hookers and brothels. He knew the area well. What if he fucked her before? Yuck. The idea of sharing a hole with Tomas made me sick. But then again Ginny probably screwed hundreds of guys, who was I kidding here?

"She said her name was Ginny."

"Hmm, don't recognise that name. She must be new. Send her my way if you see her again," said Tomas.

"Doubt it. She was pretty weird, man," I said, gulping down my own beer.

"In a good way?"

"No, not really. I'm quite sure she was the fuck of my life but she had some serious behaviour issues…"

"Oh yeah? Was she a bad girl? Did you punish her?" Tomas said, grinning.

I decided to stir the conversation elsewhere. Ginny remained a mystery and I wasn't sure what to make of the whole thing. She was mental, no doubt about that, but perhaps there was a method to her madness? Or maybe I was deluded myself?

Since puberty, I had a thing for girls who were different. Different is attractive. Tomas would disagree, I'm sure. He was an automaton who fancied stereotypical girls—models and that sort of shit. Not me. I was curious to discover what lurked under the façade—under Ginny's façade.

"You bet! Are you free tomorrow? I'm thinking about taking a day off and heading to the gym in the afternoon."

Tomas grimaced but I knew he wouldn't say no to a workout. The guy was obsessed with bodybuilding and popping steroids—whores and working out was his life. To be honest, I was surprised that he could still get his dick up after all the anabolics he injected.

"Mmm, I'm broken but sure, I'm always up for a session. Besides, training with you is a walk in a park. I'm surprised you can even lift this bottle of beer," he chuckled.

"Gimme some of that shit you're popping and I'll lift like The Hulk!"

 WALKED home from the Pump House Gym the following evening. Tomas's physical prowess knackered me out and I needed some fresh air. I felt good, though. Tired but good. I had more energy (and enthusiasm) for evening workouts. I wasn't a morning person at all and could not grasp why anyone would exercise in the morning.

Tomas was always stronger than me, even when we were kids. I was taller, at least 5 inches but also skinnier. Shorter men are able to lift more weight because their limbs are shorter, so they have a shorter distance to travel to lift the weight. Therefore their muscles have to work less hard than a tall person—basic physics. He was blessed with good genes, too, and put on muscle very easily. I swear if he only did 5 push-ups a day, he would still look buff.

His body also produced more testosterone (naturally *and* with the help of steroids). As a result, Tomas was hairier than a monkey and I still couldn't grow a full beard at the age of 32. I've seen teenage boys in town with more facial hair. At least I didn't have to shave my back or anything (unlike Tomas).

The warm spring breeze rustled my hair as I strolled through the park, sipping the protein shake from a plastic container. It tasted like vomit and I hoped that this so called "nutrition" was actually contributing towards some visible muscle growth. It cost an absolute fortune with the Government's latest 20% tax increase on all bodybuilding supplements.

I fucking despised politicians. Instead of raising prices of products for people who were trying to keep healthy and exercise, how about raising the prices of fags and booze so the alcoholics and nicotine addicts can't afford them? I never understood their logic.

Tomas explained to me on many occasions that my main problem was that I saw everything black & white, that sometimes things weren't that simple. Well, they were to me. If someone asked me a question (no matter how personal) I would give them a straight answer (even if it was a brutally honest one). I had zero tolerance for political correctness or for people who beat around the bush.

After twenty minutes of strolling, I turned into the quiet street and headed toward my dwelling. The small black gate squeaked as I pushed it open, slowly climbing the steel staircase.

"I'm so sorry about the other night," said the voice I dreaded to hear.

I looked up and saw Ginny's face, tears streaming down her pink cheeks. I couldn't see my own face but I assumed it was white as chalk. This was exactly what I feared the most, her turning up at my place. Just like that.

"What are you doing here?"

She lowered her eyes, embarrassed.

"I just wanted to apologise. I really must've freaked you out."

"Why? You don't need to apologise to me. You're a whore and I was a paying customer. Our business is done. Everybody's happy. You don't owe me anything," I replied, ignoring the rest of what she said.

Ginny pondered this for a moment. "Please, can we just talk inside?"

"No!" I exclaimed, "I'm not sure what you think is going on here but I'm not your friend, alright? I don't know you and I don't want to. You're a street whore. I made a mistake in renting out your mouth and pussy and I don't want to see you here again, got it? Now leave."

"Why are you so horrible to me? I might be a whore, but I'm still a human being," Ginny said, defending her honour with a cliché.

"You're a vermin, that's what you are. I *hate* your kind." I spat on her shiny boot.

Her reflexes were almost feline, she must've anticipated what I was about to do and moved her boot out of the way just in the nick of time. The spittle landed on my threshold instead. Shit.

"Why? Why do you hate us so much?" Ginny demanded.

"That's none of your fucking business! What do you want from me?" I said.

"I want you to get to know me. The *real* me, not Ginny. I want to show you who I really am, who Katerina is."

"And why would I want to know her? What makes you so fucking special from all the other hookers?"

Actually, I already knew she was special from the other prostitutes. Who else would decapitate a rat with their bare teeth and lick blood from the carcass? I hated whores, almost with a Jack the Ripper kind of passion, but Ginny or Katerina or whatever the fuck her name was, intrigued me. She had some kind of a gravitational pull on me, no matter how hard I tried to resist.

"Please, let's just talk inside for a minute,"

I sighed, defeated. "Fine, but you better be quick!"

"I'm no stranger to quickies," she said with a giggle.

I was regretting this already. We proceeded to the living room and I made us some coffee. I filled about a half of Ginny's mug with boiling water and the rest with cold, mixing the temperature so the coffee wasn't too hot. I wanted her to leave as soon as possible.

"There you go," I said, passing her the cup.

She took it gratefully and sipped it in silence.

"So you're real name is Katerina? Why did you tell me that?" I asked.

"Because I wanted to share something personal with you."

"More personal than your vagina?"

She smiled.

"Now it's your turn to share something personal with me. Tell me why do you hate prostitutes so much?"

I blew on my steaming coffee. "Quid pro quo, huh?"

Katerina sipped her coffee, her curious eyes studying my face.

"Fine, I'll tell you," I took a deep breath, "my mother was a whore. I never even knew who my fucking father was; I don't think she did, either."

What the hell was wrong with me? This was my darkest secret. I'd never told anyone before, not even Tomas, and here I was—openly discussing it with a strange hooker I didn't even know. Fuck.

"Sorry to hear that. That's tough. What's your name?" Katerina said.

"Don't worry about it; I don't want your sympathy. And it's Kamil," I said, trying not to sound bitter.

"That's a nice name," she said, drinking more of her coffee.

I mirrored her action, saying nothing.

"So you wanna tell me what the fuck you were doing to that rat?"

Katerina looked away then, distressed at the mention of the subject.

"After we fell asleep on the couch, I heard a noise in the kitchen. It was coming from your bin. I opened it and saw a rat there so I grabbed it and killed it for you. You witnessed the rest..." she said, as if it was perfectly natural.

"You ripped its head off with your teeth, didn't you?"

"I don't remember. Sometimes I have these episodes...these uncontrollable urges."

"You're fucking weird. I need a piss. Stay there, don't touch anything," I said, pointing at the couch and walking towards the bathroom.

I pondered Katerina's words while I aimed the stream of piss into the bowl. I could tell she was speaking in half truths. There was more to her story than that. I just needed to pry it out of her somehow. I flushed the toilet and exited from the bathroom. I could see from the hallway that the couch was empty. Where the fuck was she now?

I hastened my step and barged into the living room. Katerina was bending over, her skirt raised up, knickers wrapped around her ankles, pressing and rubbing her bare ass against the wooden leg of my table. She dug her long fingernails into the carpet, scratching, kneading. Then she let out a golden stream of piss.

I watched it unfold in a mixture of confusion and fascination.

"Stop! What are you doing? Jesus Christ! What is wrong with you?" I yelled, running into the kitchen and grabbing a wet cloth with some disinfectant.

Katerina snapped out of it and hopped to the bathroom. She came back with some toilet paper, wiping her vagina just as I was wiping her piss off the table and carpet.

"First you dine on rats in my kitchen and now you piss all over my furniture. Are you retarded or something?" I said, scrubbing hard.

"I'm really sorry, Kamil! I don't know what came over me. It happened so quickly!"

"Is your pussy so loose that your bladder is poking out and you can't control when you need to piss? You know? Like what old women suffer from, if they had six kids and whatnot? You should be wearing fucking diapers," I ranted.

"N-no, nothing like that. Please, don't be angry with me," she pleaded in a state of confusion.

I resumed scrubbing and glanced at Katerina. She was crying and trembling. For a moment, I felt sorry for her. She was damaged. I was damaged. Perhaps we could help each other.

"I'm not angry. I mean I am a little bit; I love this freakin' table but don't worry about it. You need to tell me what's wrong with you, though. Why are you behaving like this?" I pressed gently.

Katerina stood there, rooted to the carpet, frantically shaking her head from side to side. "I'm sorry...I can't!"

Then she flipped around and ran for the door. Before I could get up off my knees, the door slammed and she was gone.

HE next night, I decided to follow her. I took another day off work (perks of being your own boss) and waited for darkness to descend. When the street lamps sprang to life, I peered out of the window of my flat. If I leaned out far enough, I could just about see the corner (and whoever waited on it).

Some other whore occupied it. Damn. I made myself a cup of coffee and waited patiently. The hooker got picked up by an approaching punter in a Mercedes and disappeared out of sight. Five minutes later, another prostitute replaced her. Still—no Katerina. I began to despair. I kept spying out of the window with a sense of urgency. Where was she? Perhaps she took a night off, too? (Perks of being a hooker?).

Katerina didn't make an appearance until 1 a.m. She stood on the corner for about half an hour, flashing seductive smiles (and occasionally tits) at the passing cars. I kept popping my head in and out of the window like a fucking turtle, hoping she wouldn't see me. Then she started walking away. It seemed like she was giving up for the night. Or trying a different street. This is what I was waiting for. Motion.

I snatched the keys off the table. In the hallway, I put on my leather biker jacket and All Blacks rugby hat. It was relatively warm outside but I needed to stay incognito, yet not stick out like a sore thumb. I locked the door and headed out into the streets.

It wasn't long before I caught up with Katerina. She walked slowly, stopping now and again whenever a car swished past her. I kept out of the light, watching her every move and curious as hell where she would lead me. I sincerely hoped it wouldn't be into some fucking drug den, but let's be honest, that seemed very likely.

Now it was getting risky. Katerina strolled like a snail and at this time of night, I couldn't stay behind her forever. Police cars patrolled this area frequently so I needed to be careful just as much as Katerina. Last thing I needed was to get busted in the middle of the night, following (or in their eyes, approaching) a whore.

She turned into a dark, unlit alley. Prague was full of them and I didn't enjoy trailing her down that path. Anything could've happened in one of those. I waited, pondering whether to continue or abandon my little mission. Curiosity prevailed in the end and I stepped into the shadows of the alley. I could still make out her silhouette in the moonlight, several metres in front of me. Most of these alleys were a dead end. Where was she going?

My heart was beating like a drum. I glanced at the night sky. It was a full moon. And here I was, stalking a hooker in a dead end alley. Out of nowhere, strange fantasies started unfolding in my mind. Was she going to turn into a fucking werewolf? Would she pull out a broom out of her fucking ass and fly towards the moon? *No, no. I've seen too many horror movies.* Worst case scenario, *realistic* scenario, was that her pimp would stab me to death in this shithole alley. I shook my head in order to banish the illusions and continued walking. After a minute or two, the inevitable happened. I saw a gigantic black wall, rising in the distance. We were reaching the end of the alley.

I couldn't walk any further, not without being seen. I crouched and hid behind an elongated staircase, waiting for Katerina to do whatever she was about to do.

"Pst, pst,pst! Where are you, my babies?" Katerina called into the shadows.

I watched from my hideout, barely breathing. Katerina carried on making those weird calls and for a moment I wondered if she lost the plot. A very probable diagnosis—she ate a rat and pissed on my table after all. Now she was talking to a wall.

"Where are you? Pst, pst,pst…"

Her insanity was too much to handle. I don't know what I expected to see when I decided to follow her, but it sure as hell wasn't this shit. I was on the verge of turning around and leaving when I heard a distant "meow". I gazed back in Katerina's direction. A half a dozen cats descended from the wall and into her embrace.

"There you are! Come to mummy…"

The feline creatures entwined themselves around her feet, meowing and purring with affection. She stroked them, returning their affection with devout fascination. A broken bottle smashed behind me. I flipped around in panic.

"How much? For this one?" The stranger asked, jamming his finger on a page of some brochure.

There were three of them. Two of the men were in their early twenties, and the third, older man, perhaps in late forties. They were speaking in broken English. Tourists then—pleasure seekers with raging hard-ons.

"Gentleman, you can't buy da girl. You can only select a task, yes, and da girl you want to perform it, yes?" Said the older man, who I was guessing was the pimp.

"What do you recommend?" asked one of the lads.

"Peace Pipe, is very popular option, yes? Da best blow job of your lives," said the pimp with a chuckle.

They passed the alley and their voices faded. I stirred my attention back to Katerina but she was gone and so were the cats.

 STROLLED back through the busy streets. Even in the middle of the night, I had to evade a series of junkies and pimps. I kept my head down and started power-walking. The sooner I reached home, the better.

A bearded man with a hoody blocked my path. "Got any spare change, son?"

I pushed past him and carried on.

"I just wanted to buy a cup of soup, you asshole!" I heard in the background.

I wasn't unsympathetic towards the homeless and during the day, I'd consider helping him out, although not with money. Most of these guys were alcoholics. They'd beg you for change, claiming they were hungry and wanted to buy some soup, but any money they'd receive would be spent on cheap liquor. If anything, I would copy my grandfather.

What he used to do, whenever a homeless guy asked him for soup, was that he actually go into a shop, buy a can of soup and give that to him on the way out. He never gave them any money because he knew what they'd spend it on. He pretty much raised me. I missed my grandfather's moral lessons and hearty laughter. So damn much.

I accelerated towards home. I thought about Katerina and what she was doing in that dark alley. Surely she didn't live there? Maybe she was homeless, too? I never thought about where street whores resided. They were probably squatting in some dodgy flats with other whores and junkies, I guess. Was it a detour? Was she on her way to somewhere else? And what was with those cats?

There were still cars swishing past as I crossed the road. I glanced at my mobile. 2:45 am. I made my way past the furniture store and turned the corner.

"Bit late for a stroll, isn't it? Or were you prowling the streets in search of me and my tight pussy?" said a familiar voice, out of the shadows.

I shrieked like a little girl, startled by Katerina's unexpected ambush.

"Fuck! You scared the shit out of me! What are you doing here?" I said, leaning forward and exhaling heavily.

"That's a silly question. Hello? This is my corner? This is where I work? The question is what are you doing here in the middle of the night?"

If I wasn't so shaken up by her sudden appearance, I'd have told her to go fuck herself and mind her own business.

"You got me. I couldn't sleep so I went out for some fresh air," I lied.

Katerina arched an eyebrow. I hoped she didn't know me well enough and wasn't able to see through my lies like Tomas could.

"Is that right?" she paused for effect, "well, how about we go to your place then? I'm sure I've got something that will help you sleep."

She raised the skirt and flashed her smooth cunt.

"Sounds like a plan."

The flat was only a minute away. I didn't really fancy a fuck but was eager to find out more about my new acquaintance and her habits. I unlocked the door and gestured for her to come in. Katerina removed her boots automatically this time. I liked her more already.

"Want some coffee?" I offered.

"Yeah, sure, that'd be great."

I gave her the proper stuff from my secret Colombian stash.

"Here you go," I said, passing the mug over and sitting next to her on the couch.

"So how's business tonight?"

"Kinda slow. That's why I'm here really."

"I see. What else do you do apart from hooking?"

She gave me the are-you-serious look.

"Are you gonna fuck me or what? If you want a meaningless chit chat go to a fucking bar or something. I'm here to make money."

"You changed your tune all of a sudden. Whatever happened to 'getting to know the real you'?" I said.

She blew on her steaming coffee.

"You're the one to talk. Whatever happened to 'I'm not your friend, just a customer'?" she countered, avoiding my eyes.

"Yeah, guess I'm kind of contradicting myself here, huh? Well, what can I say? It's true, I'm not your friend, but surely we can indulge in some small talk, right?"

"Small talk won't pay for my food. You wanna talk? Fine, but let's see some money. I have an expensive ear," Katerina said, taking another sip of her coffee.

I slipped out a 500 crown note from my wallet and passed it over to her. She reached for the money, hesitating ever so slightly.

"This is a first,"

"What is?" I asked, tucking my wallet away.

"Someone paying for my ear rather than pussy,"

"I have an ear fetish, don't you know?" I said, chuckling.

"Is it really so unusual that someone would pay for your company rather than services?"

I knew this was a naïve question the second it left my mouth.

"Erm, yeah! In case you didn't notice, I'm not some fucking classy escort rich guys take to fancy restaurants! I'm street trash—the lowest of the low. I fuck sleazy old married men for a couple of crowns."

"Sorry, I wasn't trying to be clever with you. It just popped out," I said.

Katerina's description of her brutal reality had a strange effect on me. I felt something, but not sure what. Sadness? Compassion? Pity, perhaps?

"It's okay. It's not your fault. This is the path I've chosen," she said, matter-of-factly.

I caught an unpleasant aroma then, coming from my feet, realizing suddenly that I'd been wearing the same pair of socks for about a week.

"Sorry about the smell," I said, "been wearing these socks for decades."

"If it makes you feel any better, I once wore the same knickers for two weeks?"

It didn't make me feel better.

I removed the socks and squeezed them together, forming a ball. Then I aimed at the purple washing basket in the corner and attempted a shot all the way from the couch. I missed and the socks landed outside the basket. Katerina twitched, as if she was on edge all of a sudden—excited by something.

She sprinted towards the basket and picked up the socks, bringing them back to me without a word. I blinked and she sat down again.

"Erm, it's not a big deal. The socks were fine where they were. I was going to pick them up later," I said.

She giggled and I formed a little ball and chucked them at the basket. I missed again. Katerina stiffened and ran to pick the socks up, once more dropping them at my feet. I flashed an awkward smile.

"Are you suffering from OCD or what?"

I got up from the couch and walked over to the washing basket, placing the dirty socks inside. When I turned around, she still sat on the couch in a stiff manner. Her back was straight as a ruler and she kept digging her nails into the cushions. Was she having another one of her "episodes"?

"Are you hungry? I eat cheap and haven't got much but..."

"Have you got any fish?" Katerina asked.

Actually, I did. Fish were part of my diet and a great source of Omega 3. I bought them regularly—still, a strange food request from a hooker.

"Erm, I've got some mackerel in a spicy tomato sauce. Do you want some?"

"Yes, please!"

She wasn't going anywhere near my dick now with her fishy mouth, that was for sure.

Katerina wolfed down the meagre portion on the plate and I observed, quietly wondering how long it's been since her last meal. She licked her lips and smiled, full and content.

"Do you want some more? I've got some salad?"

"No, thank you. You've done enough and I'll remember your generosity in the future."

"Will I get some blow job discounts then? Buy one, get one free?" I joked.

"Maybe. Listen, what were you really doing outside? I know I'm a street whore but I'm not completely stupid."

My smile evaporated from the sudden shift of subject. I thought she fell for my lie. I was wrong. A bunch of excuses raced through my mind. Shit! What was I going to tell her?

"What do you mean? I told you, I couldn't sleep so I got up for a walk to clear my head."

"Men lie to me every night and you're a crap liar, Kamil."

Fuck! Was I really that bad at lying? Could everyone tell? Even a whore that barely knew me?

I cleared my throat.

"I...went outside... to look for you," I said.

"Why?"

"I was desperate for a fuck."

"Really? We've been chatting for the last hour. You *paid* me to talk to you. I know you don't wanna fuck tonight. Stop being a dick and tell me the truth."

"Fine! I followed you, alright? I wanted to know more about you. What you get up to, where you live – that kind of stuff."

"Why?" Katerina asked again.

"You're...intriguing. These weird "episodes" you're having, I was eager to find out more. So I followed you."

"How far?"

I drained my coffee cup. "To some fucking alley. You were surrounded by a bunch of cats."

"What else did you see?"

Her tone was deadly serious, her face solid.

"Erm, not much. You were stroking bunch of cats and then someone smashed a bottle behind me, there were a couple of tourists searching for whores and that's it. When I turned around again—you were gone."

Katerina seemed satisfied with my explanation and her shoulders relaxed.

"That's really fucking creepy, Kamil, and I'm not cool with this. I don't want some fucking stalker on my back..."

"I'm not stalking you!"

She shot me an aggressive look.

"Okay, I was—but only once!" I said, holding my arms in the air. "It won't happen again. I don't know what I was thinking. You know I'm not weird."

"Do I? I don't know anything about you apart from the fact that you sell axes and knives, which is fucking disturbing by the way, and you follow me around at night! You could be a fucking psycho! You're not gonna smell my knickers whilst you're chopping off my head, are you?"

"The ones you wore for two weeks? Please..." I said, feeling the heat rising to my face.

"The only psycho in this room is you! You're the one tearing heads off rats! Pleasuring yourself on my table and pissing on it! Who does that? Don't fucking turn this around on me! You're the weird one."

"You know what? I don't need this shit. Stay the fuck away from me and find a different pussy to fuck." Katerina said, putting on her jacket.

"Look, you're overreacting. Let's just sit back down and talk about this," I offered.

"Is this the part where you declare your mad love for me?"

"Pfft, you wish!"

"You're obsessed with me, Kamil."

"Don't flatter yourself."

"Stay away from me then."

"Oh, don't worry—I will from now on. Just don't come back begging when you're desperate."

Katerina turned around and walked to the hallway, not saying another word. I didn't follow her. I waited for the sound of the door. When she left, I stretched out on the couch. The clock on the wall showed 4:47 am. I was up all night and still felt restless. Nearly a week went by since we met and I was no closer to unlocking the enigma that was Katerina. And after this night, it seemed like she would remain a mystery forever.

HE sat in my Skoda, four days after the alley pursuit and our bitter exchange of angry words. I decided to give her some space, let her cool down. Eventually, she would crawl back to me—for the right price of course. Katerina was the desperate one in this twisted relationship and I knew she wouldn't stay away for long.

"Blowjob or a fuck?" she asked, "I don't offer anal."

"Straight to business, huh? No hello or how you been?"

Katerina smirked. "Fuck off, Kamil. I don't have time for this. Let's not pretend any more. You're not my friend, just another trick, yeah? I'm a whore and you will always despise me for that, so let's get this over with. What's it gonna be? A fuck or a blowjob?"

I pondered her words for a moment and knew she was right. My hatred for Katerina's kind would never fade (thanks to my cunt of a mother). She intrigued me with her peculiar behaviour, and I yearned to get at the bottom of it, but at the end of the day—I felt nothing for her. I offered my "friendship" only to satisfy my own, selfish curiosity.

"Have it your way," I said.

"What's it gonna be then?"

"Suck it a little first, followed by a fuck. We'll work out the price after. You cool with that?"

Katerina nodded and her trust unsettled me. She tied her hair back in a rubber band and leaned across to the driver seat. I unzipped my jeans.

"Wait. That's it? You just gonna take my word for it? What happened to money up front?"

"You treated me nicely so far and earned some trust, but hit me or fuck me over in any way and that will be the last time you'll ever have this pussy," she said, pointing at her crotch.

"Fair enough."

I knew her threats were empty. As long as I waved a 500 crown note in front of her face, she would always come running. Such was the nature of her profession.

While she worked on my cock with her lips, I reminisced about how vacant my life really was. At 32 years old, I was barely making a living, renting an old flat in a scummy neighbourhood surrounded by brothels and lowlifes. I had no lasting relationships to be proud of, no kids to pass my wisdom onto (if I had any) and here I was, getting my dick sucked by a deranged cat lady/whore in my tiny car. This pathetic self-admission did nothing for my hard-on so instead, I leaned back and focused on Katerina's pierced tongue tickling my helmet.

"That'll do," I said, lifting her head up, "I don't want to come in your mouth, as tempting as it is. Take your knickers off and let's fuck."

"I don't have any on," Katerina said.

She licked her palm and lubricated her pussy with it. I rolled my pants down half way and she climbed on top of me. This was fucking awkward and uncomfortable. I never shagged anyone in a car before. Now I knew it was for a reason. I struggled to find her cunt so Katerina reached down and with her skilled hand, guided me inside her. She was still slippery from her spit and I moaned with pleasure as her ass slapped against my cock and balls.

Katerina increased her rhythm, bouncing faster and faster, nearing her climax. And then something very strange happened. As she reached her orgasm, she arched her back and dug her sharp nails into my thighs. I let out a yelp but wasn't ready at the sound that erupted from her lips. It terrified me. She produced what sounded like a deep, primal meow. She fucking *meowed* in my lap! I shoved her off my dick and back into the passenger seat.

"What the fuck are you? Some kind of a cat mutant?" I shouted, too distressed by the situation to care if anyone heard us outside the car.

Katerina stared at me, not blinking.

"Look, this shit has gone on far enough! You better start talking!"

She pulled her skirt down, trying to buy time.

"Well? Don't test me, Katerina! You owe me an explanation after witnessing all of this!"

She chewed on her lower lip, locked in an internal struggle with herself. After a moment, she began to talk.

"Okay…I'll tell you. You were open enough with me to talk about your mother and your hatred for whores, so it's only fair I'm open with you about my illness."

"So you are ill?" I blurted out, "what exactly are we talking here? Are you crazy?"

She smiled a heavy-hearted sort of smile.

"No, although I can see why you would come to that conclusion," she said.

"Go on," I encouraged her.

"I was born with an extremely rare mental disorder, called *Galeanthropy*."

"Gale-what?"

"Galeanthropy."

"What the fuck is that?"

"It's a mental condition of thinking that one has become a cat by adopting feline mannerisms and habits. At least that's what the doctor told me when I was little," Katerina said.

I raised my eyebrows, struggling to take it in. At last, it all started falling into place. This bizarre revelation explained Katerina's "hunt" for the rat, kneading my carpet and rubbing her ass on the table, her meowing, playing fetch with the socks, even her adoration for cats in the alley. She lived her life by thinking she was a cat so cats were the only friends she kept.

"Do you understand now?"

I nodded, not knowing what else to say—except how pissed off I felt that she ruined my orgasm.

"How much do I owe you?" I said in the end.

"Shall we say a 1000?"

I gave her 2000.

"What's this for?"

"Future services," I said.

Katerina beamed. Her smile was genuine this time, stretching from ear to ear. I could tell that she was grateful. Not just for the money, but for my kindness—for my acceptance. I still didn't know what to make of the whole thing. Was I truly obsessed with her? Only time would tell.

"See you around?"

I nodded as she climbed out of the car with feline dexterity. Then I watched her descend into the creeping darkness of the city.

Dear reader,

We hope you enjoyed reading *Katerina*. Please take a moment to leave a review, even if it's a short one. Your opinion is important to us.

Discover more books by Erik Hofstatter at
https://www.nextchapter.pub/authors/erik-hofstatter

Want to know when one of our books is free or discounted? Join the newsletter at http://eepurl.com/bqqB3H.

Best regards,
Erik Hofstatter and the Next Chapter Team

Katerina
ISBN: 978-4-86752-235-6

Published by
Next Chapter
1-60-20 Minami-Otsuka
170-0005 Toshima-Ku, Tokyo
+818035793528
27th July 2021

Lightning Source UK Ltd.
Milton Keynes UK
UKHW010748110821
388656UK00001B/193